Some other titles

The Baked Bean Kids
by Ann Pilling / Derek Matthews

Beware Olga!
by Gillian Cross / Arthur Robins

The Haunting of Pip Parker
by Anne Fine / Emma Chichester Clark

Holly and the Skyboard
by Ian Whybrow/ Tony Kenyon

Little Luis and the Bad Bandit
by Ann Jungman / Russell Ayto

Millie Morgan, Pirate
by Margaret Ryan / Caroline Church

A Night to Remember
by Dyan Sheldon / Robert Crowther

Sky Watching
by Dyan Sheldon / Graham Percy

DICK KING-SMITH

THE FINGER EATER

Illustrations by Arthur Robins

WALKER BOOKS
AND SUBSIDIARIES
LONDON • BOSTON • SYDNEY

For Gareth
A.R.

First published 1992 by
Walker Books Ltd, 87 Vauxhall Walk
London SE11 5HJ

This edition published 1994

12 14 15 13 11

Text © 1992 Fox Busters Ltd
Illustrations © 1992 Arthur Robins

Printed in Great Britain by The Guernsey Press Co. Ltd

British Library Cataloguing in Publication Data
A catalogue record for this book is
available from the British Library.

ISBN 0-7445-3091-1

CONTENTS

CHAPTER 1

Long long ago, in the cold lands
of the North, there lived a most
unusual troll.

9

Like all the hill-folk (so called
because they usually made their
homes in holes in the hills) he was
hump-backed and bow-legged,
with a frog-face and bat-ears and
razor-sharp teeth.

But he grew up (though, like all
other trolls, not very tall) with an
extremely bad habit –

he liked to eat fingers!

Ulf (for that was his name) always
went about this in the same way.

Whenever he spied someone
walking alone on the hills, he would
come up, smiling broadly, and hold
out a hand, and say politely:

"How do you do?"

Now trolls are usually rude and extremely grumpy and don't care how anyone does, so the person would be pleasantly surprised at meeting such a jolly one, and would hold out his or her hand to shake Ulf's.

Then Ulf would take it and, quick
as a flash, bite off a finger with his
razor-sharp teeth and run away as
fast as his bow-legs would carry
him, chewing like mad and grinning
all over his frog-face.

15

Strangers visiting those parts were amazed to see how many men, women and children were lacking a finger on their right hands, especially children, because their fingers were more tender and much sought after by Ulf.

Nobody lacked more than one finger, because even small children weren't foolish enough to shake hands if they met Ulf a second time, but ran away with them deep in their pockets.

Bother!

It was usually the index finger
that Ulf nipped off because it was
the easiest to get at, so that many
children grew up pointing with a
middle finger...

and holding a pencil between
middle and third...

but sometimes Ulf went for the little
one: thumbs, for some reason, he
did not seem to fancy.

Strangely, the people of those
lands were tolerant and long-
suffering and seemed to put up with
Ulf's bad habit.

"What can't be cured must be endured," they would say, and since they considered it was no use crying over spilt milk, they wasted no tears over lost fingers but got on with their lives with only seven.

CHAPTER 2

Who knows how long Ulf the troll
might have continued in his wicked
ways if it had not been for a little
girl named Gudrun.

Gudrun was the only child of a reindeer farmer. She had golden hair which she wore in a long plait, and eyes the colour of cornflowers.

Indeed she was as pretty as a picture, looking as though reindeer butter wouldn't melt in her mouth.

She was also a sensible child, who paid attention to what her parents told her.

One evening, as they all sat round the fire outside their tent, Gudrun's mother said to her:

Remember, you must never shake hands with a troll.

She stirred the cooking-pot that was suspended above the flames. The hand that held the ladle had no little finger.

With his right hand, on which the index finger was missing, Gudrun's father picked up a stick to put on the fire.

"But why," said Gudrun, "didn't either of you do that?"

"When we were both children," said her mother, "we didn't know about the Finger-eater."

"We were among the first in this district," said her father, "to lose a finger. But now everybody knows."

"Why don't all the mothers and fathers warn their children then?" said Gudrun.

"They do," said her mother, "but sometimes the children don't listen, or they just forget. Mind you remember."

Gudrun thought deeply about
this while she was out on the hills,
helping her father herd his reindeer
as they grazed their way across
the slopes.

It's all very well, she thought, to tell children not to get their fingers eaten, but someone ought to tell that troll not to eat them. Eating people's fingers is wrong.

And being not only a very pretty but also a very resolute child, she resolved that she would stop the Finger-eater. But how?

"Father," she said as she sat milking one of the reindeer, "how big is a troll?"

"No taller than you, Gudrun," her father said, "but much much stronger."

"Have you ever met one?"

For answer her father held up
his right hand.

"Oh yes," said Gudrun. "But since then, I mean?"

"No," said her father, "but I have quite often seen the hill-folk, just for

a moment. Then they scuttle down
their holes, for they are all shy of
people. Except Ulf the Finger-eater."

"You have never seen him again?"

"No, and nor will you, I hope."

But not long after, Gudrun did.

CHAPTER 3

Even in those bleak Northern lands
there are days in the short summer
which are bright and warm and
flower-filled, and on such a morning

Gudrun's father handed her a flask.
It was made of reindeer skin, was
this flask, and it was stopped with a
cork made out of reindeer
horn, and it was
filled with fresh,
rich reindeer
milk.

"Be a good girl and take this to your mother," her father said, for the herd's grazing grounds were not far from the family tent, and it did not occur to him that she might come to any harm.

Gudrun set off across the hill,
carrying the flask in her right hand.
Before she had gone far she saw,
in a steep bank, a large hole.

Could that be the home of one of
the hill-folk? she thought, and no
sooner had she thought it than out
of the hole came a hump-backed,
bow-legged figure with a frog-face
and bat-ears.

Straight towards her he came, his mouth agape in a friendly smile, his hand outstretched. "How do you do?" he said politely.

The Finger-eater! thought Gudrun and she remembered her parents' advice to put her hands in her pockets and run. But I won't, she said to herself bravely, for now may be my only chance to make the Finger-eater see how wrong it is to eat fingers. So she stood her ground.

"I'm sorry," she said, "but I cannot shake your hand because I'm holding this flask of milk."

"You could always hold it with your other hand," said Ulf, for it was he.

41

"I could," said Gudrun, "but I won't. I've heard of you, you see. You are Ulf the Finger-eater."

"Well, well," said Ulf, passing his tongue across his razor-sharp teeth, "and what is your name, little girl?"

"It's Gudrun. Now let me tell you something, Ulf," she said. "Eating fingers is wrong."

A clever little miss, thought Ulf. How can I trick her? He sat down on a nearby tree-stump, and crossed one bow-leg over the other, looking serious and thoughtful.

"You're right, Gudrun," he said.
"I'm wrong to eat people's fingers,
I see that now. But at least give me
a drink of milk."

And when she holds out the
flask, he thought, I'll soon have one
of those lovely little pink sausages!

"Not on your life," said Gudrun. "Thanks to you, both my mother and my father are short of a finger."

"How time flies!" said Ulf. "That must have been when I was a very young troll. I've probably had a hundred fingers since then."

"Well, you're not having a hundred and one," said Gudrun, "but on second thoughts I'll give you that drink," and pulling out the cork, she jerked the flask so that the milk shot out straight into Ulf's frog-face, and as he stood gasping, she dashed away.

CHAPTER 4

Gudrun did not tell her parents
of her meeting with Ulf. She simply
said she had tripped, the cork had
come out of the flask, and the milk
had all spilled (a white lie, she
told herself).

But she continued to think long
and hard about the Finger-eater.
Somehow or other he must be
made to give up his horrid habit.

Then one day Gudrun had a
sudden, brilliant idea.

She was sitting outside the family
tent, playing with a reindeer antler.
This was the time of year when all
the reindeer (for the cows are
horned as well as the bulls) shed
their antlers before growing fresh

ones, and they were lying about
everywhere. Hard as iron they
were, and many of them were of
the strangest shapes, for reindeer
antlers are very large and many-
pointed, those of some of the
bulls curving right round
and down until they
almost meet the
animals' faces.

The single antler that Gudrun held was quite a small one, probably from a young beast, but at its tip it had an odd shape, something like a human hand. It had at its end a flat surface resembling the palm of a hand and from this surface five points protruded. Just like four fingers and a thumb, thought Gudrun, and that was when the idea hit her.

That afternoon Ulf emerged from
his hole to see Gudrun approaching,
her long blonde plait swinging as
she walked, her cornflower-blue
eyes sparkling, her right hand, much
to the troll's surprise, already
outstretched in greeting. Admittedly
she was wearing a large pair of
reindeer hide gloves, but those
won't save her, thought Ulf.

He advanced to meet her.

"Hello, Ulf," said Gudrun brightly.
"I've come to say I'm sorry for
throwing the milk at you. Will you
shake hands and then we can be
friends?"

Stupid child, thought Ulf. She's
asking for it. This time I won't just
have one finger, I'll have all four,
and he grabbed Gudrun's right hand
and shoved it into his frog-mouth
and bit it as hard as he could.

Then Ulf's great cry of agony echoed and rang from the circling hills, as his razor-sharp teeth broke and smashed and shattered, every one.

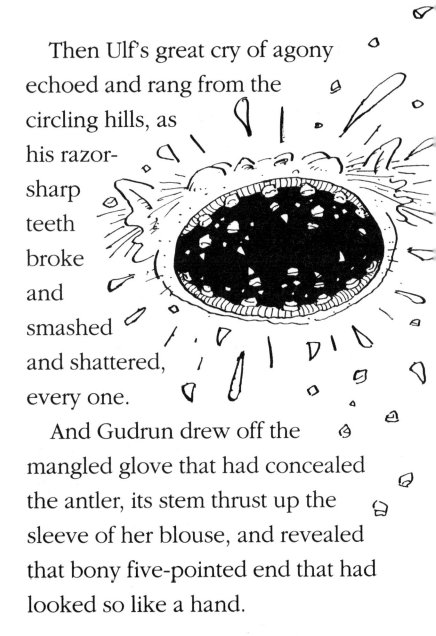

And Gudrun drew off the mangled glove that had concealed the antler, its stem thrust up the sleeve of her blouse, and revealed that bony five-pointed end that had looked so like a hand.

"Hard luck, Ulf," she said. "You bit off more than you could chew."

"Oh! Oh!" moaned the Finger-eater. "My teeth! My teeth! Every single one is loose in my head! Oh, it is agony! Help me! Help me!"

"I will," said Gudrun, and she took from the pocket of her skirt a pair of stout pliers, a useful tool with which her father was wont to draw stones that had lodged deep between the great splay hooves of his reindeer.

"Open wide, Ulf," she said, "and I'll make you a much better troll."

Then with the pliers she pulled out the teeth of the Finger-eater, one by one, till none were left.

Chapter 5

Even after that, Ulf could not
easily rid himself of his bad habit.

Once his mouth was no longer sore, he still tried several times to live up to his name, but thanks to Gudrun, he could not. For though the reindeer can grow new antlers, hill-folk cannot grow new teeth, and those few people whose hands he caught only giggled at the harmless pressure of his toothless gums upon their fingers and told him not to be such a silly old troll.

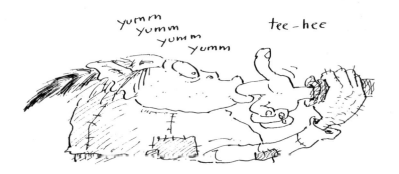

So that before long Ulf fell into a
terrible sulk, and disappeared down
his hole in the hill, and was never
seen again.

And even today, if you travel in the cold old North and stay amongst the reindeer people, you may hear the tale of the troll named Ulf and the girl called Gudrun, and how she and she alone put paid to the wicked ways of the Finger-eater.

MORE WALKER SPRINTERS
For You to Enjoy

☐ 0-7445-3188-8   *Beware Olga!*
                           by Gillian Cross/Arthur Robins   £3.50

☐ 0-7445-3103-9   *Art, You're Magic!*
                           by Sam McBratney/
                           Tony Blundell   £3.50

☐ 0-7445-3173-X   *Jolly Roger*
                           by Colin McNaughton   £3.50

☐ 0-7445-6306-2   *Little Luis and the Bad Bandit*
                           by Ann Jungman/Russell Ayto   £3.50

☐ 0-7445-3095-4   *Millie Morgan, Pirate*
                           by Margaret Ryan/
                           Caroline Church   £3.50

☐ 0-7445-5241-9   *Fort Biscuit*
                           by Lesley Howarth/
                           Ann Kronheimer   £3.50

☐ 0-7445-3183-7   *The Baked Bean Kids*
                           by Ann Pilling/
                           Derek Matthews   £3.50

Name _____

Address _____

_____